Larry Gets Lost in Alaska

Illustrated by John Skewes
Written by Michael Mullin and John Skewes

SASQUATCH BOOKS
SEATTLE

For V.C. Mas

Thanks Don, Bob, and Nancy

Manufactured in China by C&C Offset Printing Co. Ltd. Shenzhen,
Guangdong Province, in August 2012

Published by Sasquatch Books

17 16 15 14 13 12   13 12 11 10 9 8 7 6 5 4 3 2 1

Hardcover Edition, Sasquatch Books, 2011

Book design: Mint Design
Book composition: Sarah Plein

Library of Congress Cataloging-in-Publication Data is available.

ISBN-13: 978-1-57061-859-8 (paperback)   ISBN-13: 978-1-57061-728-7 (hardcover)

www.larrygetslost.com

SASQUATCH BOOKS
1904 Third Avenue, Suite 710
Seattle, WA 98101
(206) 467-4300
www.sasquatchbooks.com
custserv@sasquatchbooks.com

This is **Larry.** This is **Pete.**

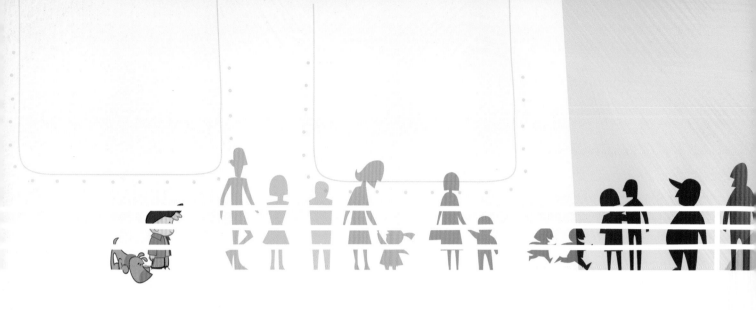

They looked out to sea, a ship's deck at their feet.

Splashing out of the water was a giant tail,
So big it could only belong to a whale.

Larry saw other creatures looking up at him.
Were they dogs enjoying an icy swim?

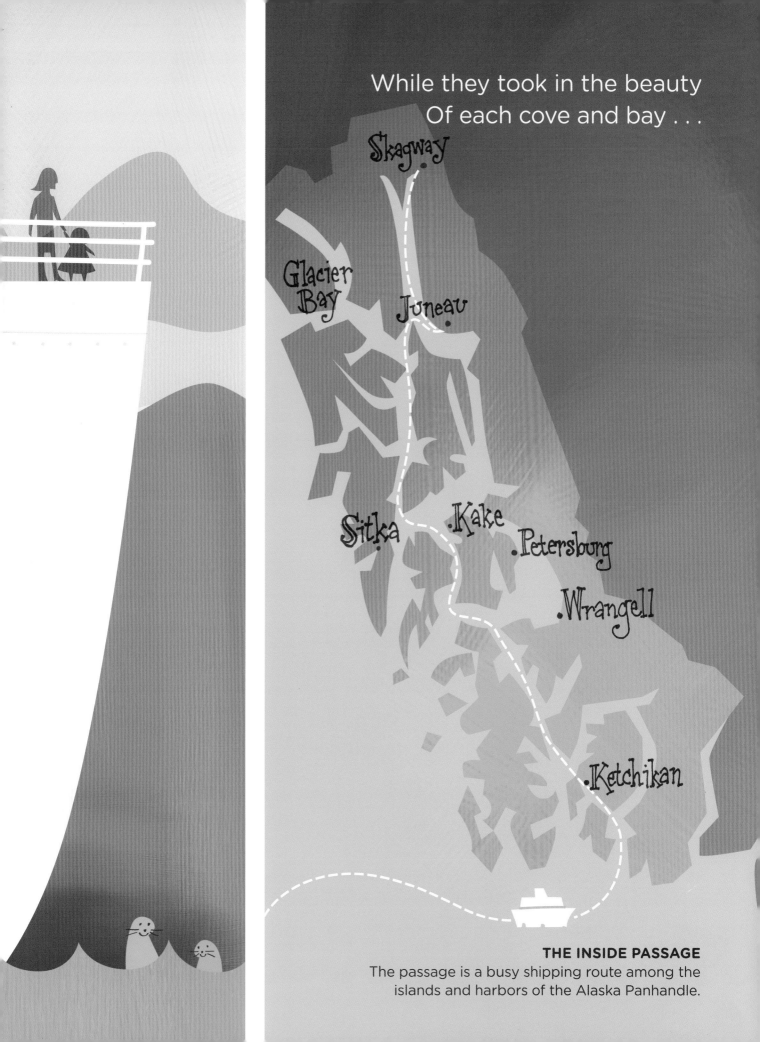

While they took in the beauty
Of each cove and bay . . .

Skagway

Glacier Bay

Juneau

Sitka

Kake

Petersburg

Wrangell

Ketchikan

THE INSIDE PASSAGE
The passage is a busy shipping route among the
islands and harbors of the Alaska Panhandle.

KETCHIKAN

JUNEAU

TOTEM PARKS
The Tlingit (KLING-kit) people, native to the Inside Passage, are known for their beautiful totem poles carved from tree trunks.

STATE CAPITAL
Juneau has no roads leading to it. The city of about 31,000 people can only be reached by water or by air.

SKAGWAY

WHITE PASS AND YUKON ROUTE
This narrow-gauge railroad was built in 1898 for gold rush prospectors on their way to the Yukon.

. . . They stopped in three
Places along the way.

There were carved wooden
Animals built in stacks.
A tram rose up high, while old
Trains rolled on tracks.

When they saw a huge
Ice chunk crash into the sea,
Larry's look said:
"Honest. That wasn't me."

ANCHORAGE

It was then time to borrow a car and ride.
The first friend they met would not fit inside.

LAKE HOOD
One of the busiest seaplane bases in the world, Lake Hood averages 190 flights a day.

GLACIER BAY

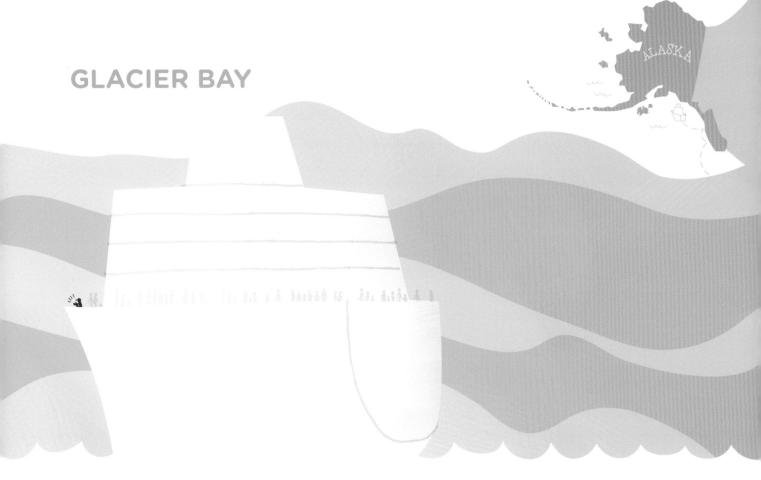

Pete's favorite part of the trip
They had planned
Was watching the seaplanes
Take off and land.

Pete was so thrilled with
The flying display,

He didn't notice a scent
Had lured Larry away.

As a man loaded boxes
Of food on board,

The pup followed,
Hoping for a treat
in reward.

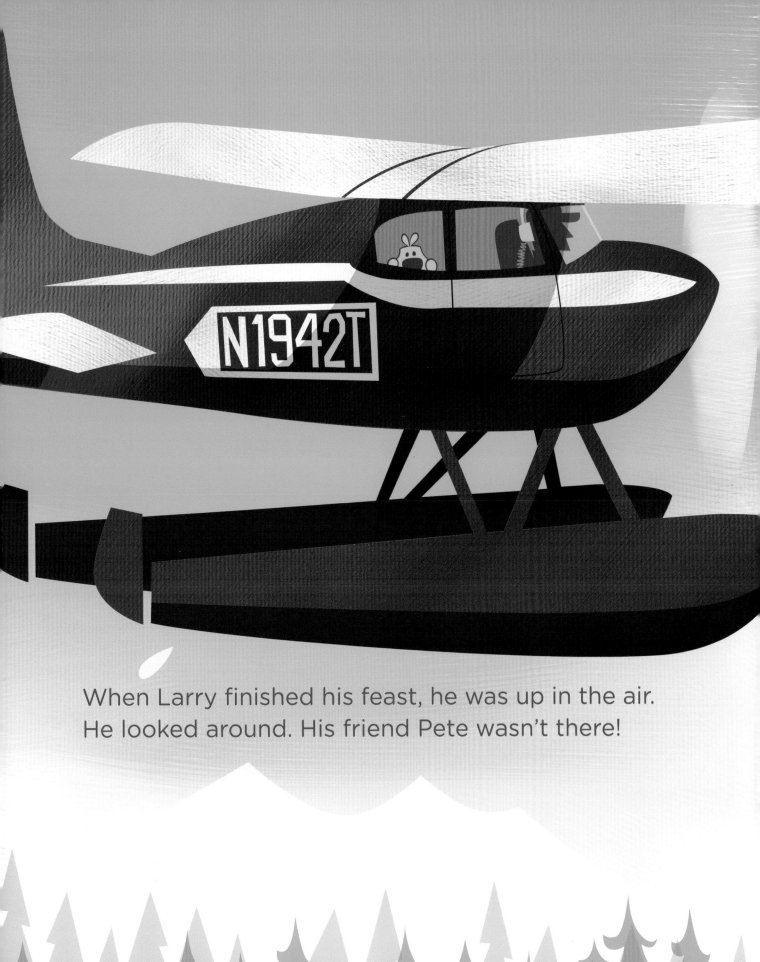

When Larry finished his feast, he was up in the air.
He looked around. His friend Pete wasn't there!

The plane went from air,
To water, to ground. . . .

Was Pete on this island?
Larry went to look around.

STAR OF KODIAK

KODIAK BEARS
There are brown bears
all over Alaska, but the
biggest live on Kodiak.
The largest ever weighed
around 1,800 pounds!

But what he found
Was a big mother bear.

Larry was more than happy
To get out of there!

Larry ran from the woods and
Dove into the sea.
But a **HUGE** friend had no clue
Where Pete might be.

WHALES
Most whales can stay underwater
without taking a breath for 10 to 30 minutes.
Some can swim up to 40 miles per hour.

But before he could see just
How far he could get . . .

. . . He felt himself hoisted
Up high in a net!

FISHING
Dutch Harbor is home to the largest
commercial fishing port in the U.S.

BALD EAGLES
Common in Alaska, the bald eagle is
the official bird of the U.S.

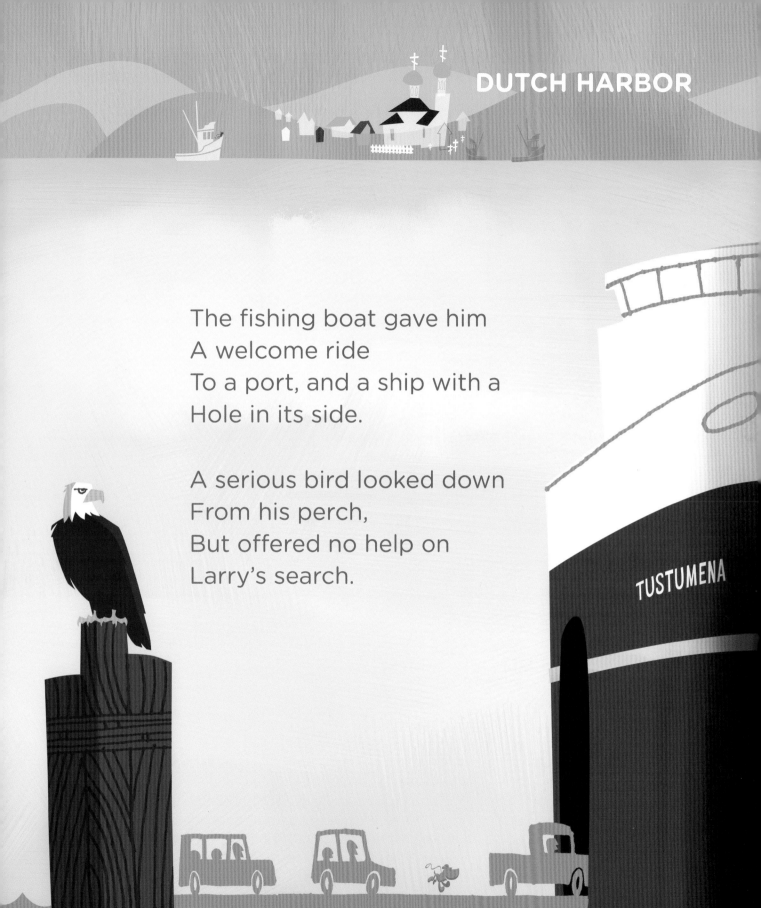

The fishing boat gave him
A welcome ride
To a port, and a ship with a
Hole in its side.

A serious bird looked down
From his perch,
But offered no help on
Larry's search.

TUSTUMENA

PIONEER PARK
Opened in 1967, this landmark contains historic cabins, an aircraft museum, a stern-wheeler, and a small railroad.

NORTH POLE, ALASKA
This small town near Fairbanks is decorated for Christmas all year. Each year the post office receives hundreds of thousands of letters addressed to Santa.

Meanwhile, Mom and Dad and Pete
Found a park with log cabins lining the street.

Close by was an interesting kind of town
That looked like Christmas all year round.

They searched for Larry high and low,
Then boarded a train, as it started to snow.

ALASKA

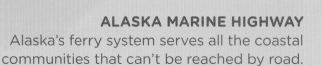

ALASKA MARINE HIGHWAY
Alaska's ferry system serves all the coastal
communities that can't be reached by road.
Boats carry people, vehicles, and freight.

From Larry's boat,
The scenery was pleasing,
But the temperature had fallen
To well below freezing.

On the boat was a truck filled
With dogs who looked strong.
They opened their door
And let Larry tag along.

At the dogs' place were
Houses and plenty to eat.
Larry saw each new friend
Had warm socks on his feet.

There weren't any extras,
But they did find instead
An old woolen hat that
Fit Larry's cold head.

When he realized the day
Had come to an end,
Larry sadly lay down.
He still missed his best friend.

One day the dogs woke up
So excited to **GO!**
They all jumped in the truck,
And drove hours through the snow.

But Larry got sleepy
As flakes fell all around.
He found a warm place to nap
And couldn't hear a sound.

And Pete was also feeling
Worried and sad.
They'd search again tomorrow,
Promised Mom and Dad.

Larry woke to an amazing, dazzling sight.
The nighttime sky was filled with light.

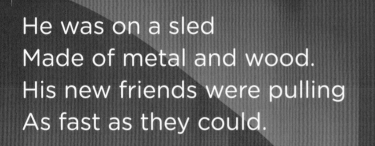

He was on a sled
Made of metal and wood.
His new friends were pulling
As fast as they could.

The driver yelled "Haw!" to turn left,
And "Gee!" to turn right.
The dog team ran silently
Into the night.

NORTHERN LIGHTS
The Aurora Borealis are natural lights in the sky,
visible near the polar regions and caused by
particles in the earth's magnetic field.

NOME

ANCHORAGE
END OF IDITAROD
NOME

Welcome
to
NOME
INC. 1901

They came to a stop in a
Loud, cheering place.
It seemed they had won
Some big, popular race.

1049
SLED DOG RACE
MILES

IDITAROD TRAIL SLED DOG RACE
The Iditarod is the most popular sporting event in Alaska. Every March more than 50 mushers and more than 1,000 dogs attempt the roughly 1,100-mile race from Anchorage to Nome. The course takes from 9 to 15 days to complete.

That's when the sled driver
Saw Larry pop up.
She asked herself,
"Who is this little pup?"

She called Pete, and a bark was
All Larry could say.
On the other end Pete was
Heard yelling, "Hooray!"

A pilot took the family
North for a while.
"How'd he get this far?"
Pete asked Mom and Dad with a smile.

POLAR BEARS
The world's largest land carnivore, an adult
male polar bear can weigh 1,500 pounds!

From his window Pete saw people waiting below.
The plane made a landing with skis on the snow.

Larry and his family were together again.
And Pete got to meet all of Larry's new friends.

On the plane ride back, **Pete** and **Larry** buckled in,
Then fell right to sleep. What a trip it had been!